T4-BAF-865

No Biting!
by Karen Katz

Grosset & Dunlap
An Imprint of Penguin Group (USA) Inc.

ISBN 978-0-448-45581-5   10 9 8

No biting your friends!
What can you bite?

Apples!

No hitting Mommy!
What can you hit?

A drum!

No pushing in line!
What can you push?

A swing!

No kicking the dog!
What can you kick?

A ball!

No spitting at your brother!

When can you spit?

When you brush your teeth!

Can you remember?

Yes, I can!